The Very Worst
Wizard

by Elizabeth Dale and Denis Cristo

FRANKLIN WATTS
LONDON • SYDNEY

Max loved being a wizard.

He loved going to Wizard School
and doing spells.

He also liked helping his wizard friends.

On Monday, Mr Whizzyfizz
had some news for the wizards.

"It's the Magic Awards this week.
The competition will start tomorrow.
I want you all to bring some
pepper dust to school," he said.

Max really wanted to win an award.

On Tuesday, Max couldn't wait to start.
Everyone began to mix their potion.

"Add your pepper dust now!"
said Mr Whizzyfizz.

"Oh no! I forgot to bring it," said Adam.

"Here, have some of mine," said Max.

But there was none left for him.

Adam's potion went green.

Max's potion did not.

"Drip some potion on your paper,"

said Mr Whizzyfizz.

"See what happens."

Adam gasped.

His paper turned into a frog!

Max's paper just went soggy.

On Wednesday, it was the flying test.

Rob's broomstick flew away!

It went up into a tree.

Max ran to get it down for Rob.

Max got stuck in the tree.

He could not get down in time

for the flying test.

"Fly, broomstick, fly!"

shouted his friends.

Off they flew around the field.

Max watched them.

He was very sad.

On Thursday, the children were making spells to grow strawberries. Max wanted to make a good spell. He said just the right things to make his strawberry plant start to grow.

"Max," Sam said, "can you help me?

I've forgotten the spell.

What do I say next?"

Max went to help Sam.

He told Sam what to say

to make her strawberry plant grow.

It grew bigger and bigger.

But Max forgot all about his spell.

His strawberry plant didn't grow at all.

He was sad.

He was not going to win an award.

Friday was the day of the Magic Awards.

Mr Whizzyfizz gave the winners

a big cup.

Adam got the award for

the best magic potion.

Rob was the best at flying.

Sam made the best spell.

Max cheered and clapped his friends.

"And now," said Mr Whizzyfizz,

"Max, will you please come up here."

"Oh no!" Max said to himself.

"I must be the very worst wizard.

My magic did not work.

Maybe I'll have to leave Magic School."

"Max, your potion went wrong,"
said Mr Whizzyfizz. "You couldn't fly,
and your strawberry spell didn't work.

But this happened because

you were always helping your friends.

So you win the best award of all.

Award for the Kindest Wizard."

Max was very happy.

He had won an award.

"That's magic!" he said.

Story order

Look at these 5 pictures and captions.
Put the pictures in the right order
to retell the story.

1

Mr FizzyWhizz calls Max to the front.

2

Max wins an award after all.

3

Max joins Wizard School.

4

Max's potion does not work.

5

Max's strawberry does not grow.

Independent Reading

This series is designed to provide an opportunity for your child to read on their own. These notes are written for you to help your child choose a book and to read it independently.

In school, your child's teacher will often be using reading books which have been banded to support the process of learning to read. Use the book band colour your child is reading in school to help you make a good choice. *The Very Worst Wizard* is a good choice for children reading at Turquoise Band in their classroom to read independently.

The aim of independent reading is to read this book with ease, so that your child enjoys the story and relates it to their own experiences.

About the book

Max is learning to be a wizard at Wizard School. He's so busy helping his friends, he keeps messing up his own spells. How can he ever win a Magic Award?

Before reading

Help your child to learn how to make good choices by asking:
"Why did you choose this book? Why do you think you will enjoy it?"
Look at the cover together and ask: "What do you think the story will be about?" Ask your child to think of what they already know about the story context. Then ask your child to read the title aloud. Ask: "What sort of wizard is the story about? What do wizards usually do?"
Remind your child that they can sound out the letters to make a word if they get stuck.
Decide together whether your child will read the story independently or read it aloud to you.

During reading

Remind your child of what they know and what they can do independently. If reading aloud, support your child if they hesitate or ask for help by telling the word. If reading to themselves, remind your child that they can come and ask for your help if stuck.

After reading

Support comprehension by asking your child to tell you about the story. Use the story order puzzle to encourage your child to retell the story in the right sequence, in their own words. The correct sequence can be found on the next page.

Help your child think about the messages in the book that go beyond the story and ask: "Do you think Max deserved to win an award? Why/Why not?

What things do you forget to do?"

Give your child a chance to respond to the story: "Did you have a favourite part? Did you think that Max learnt anything at the end of the story?"

Extending learning

Help your child understand the story structure by using the same sentence patterning and adding different elements. "Let's make up a new story about magic spells. What about a genie who grants three wishes. What wishes could he/she be asked to grant? What could go wrong with the wishes? How would the genie put it right?"

In the classroom, your child's teacher may be teaching about punctuation. Ask your child to identify some question marks and exclamation marks in the story and then ask them to practise reading the whole sentences with appropriate expression.

Franklin Watts
First published in Great Britain in 2018
by The Watts Publishing Group

Series Editors: Jackie Hamley and Melanie Palmer
Series Advisors: Dr Sue Bodman and Glen Franklin
Series Designer: Peter Scoulding

A CIP catalogue record for this book is
available from the British Library.

ISBN 978 1 4451 6218 8 (hbk)
ISBN 978 1 4451 6219 5 (pbk)
ISBN 978 1 4451 6220 1 (library ebook)

Printed in China

Franklin Watts
An imprint of
Hachette Children's Group
Part of The Watts Publishing Group
Carmelite House
50 Victoria Embankment
London EC4Y 0DZ

An Hachette UK Company
www.hachette.co.uk

www.franklinwatts.co.uk

Answer to Story order: 3, 4, 5, 1, 2